Investi GATORS
High-Rise Hijinks

This book belongs to

....

InvestiGATORS

High-Rise Hijinks

created by
John Patrick Green

additional writing by **Christopher Hastings**

illustrated by **Pat Lewis**

with layouts by **John Patrick Green**

MACMILLAN CHILDREN'S BOOKS

For the readers

This edition published in the UK 2024 by Macmillan Children's Books
an imprint of Pan Macmillan
The Smithson, 6 Briset Street, London EC1M 5NR
EU representative: Macmillan Publishers Ireland Ltd, 1st Floor,
The Liffey Trust Centre, 117–126 Sheriff Street Upper, Dublin 1, D01 YC43
Associated companies throughout the world
www.panmacmillan.com

ISBN 978-1-0350-3486-4

Copyright © John Patrick Green 2024

The right of John Patrick Green to be identified as the
author and illustrator of this work has been asserted by him
in accordance with the Copyright, Designs and Patents Act 1988.

1 3 5 7 9 8 6 4 2

A CIP catalogue record for this book is available from the British Library.

Printed and bound by CPI Group (UK) Ltd, Croydon CR0 4YY

World Book Day® and the associated logo are the registered
trademarks of World Book Day® Limited.

Registered charity number 1079257 (England and Wales).
Registered company number 03783095 (UK).

With thanks to Holmen Paper and Gould Paper Sales for their support

WORLD BOOK DAY®

World Book Day's mission is to offer every child and young person the opportunity to read and love books by giving you the chance to have a book of your own.

To find out more, and for fun activities including video stories, audiobooks and book recommendations, visit **worldbookday.com**

World Book Day is a charity sponsored by National Book Tokens.

The city in the dead of night...

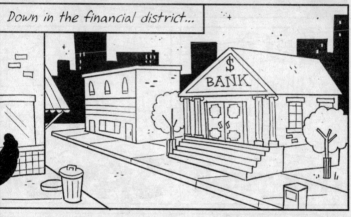

Down in the financial district...

...a shadowy figure...

1

I've heard of a floating transaction, but **THIS** is ridiculous!

Who **is** this **midnight miscreant?**

Where are they taking the bank? **HOW** are they taking the bank?

And can these questions be answered by the...

INVESTIGATORS!

Mango! Brash! Report to **S.U.I.T.*** Headquarters *ON THE DOUBLE!*

We're already on the double, boss...

...a DOUBLE-DECKER BUS!

COLE'S LAW: THE MUSICAL!

*Special Undercover Investigation Teams

Oh! I see – *LOOK OUT!* There's a **stop light** ahead!

I'll just use this **remote** in my V.E.S.T.* to turn the light green!

ZAP!

Um...

I can't tell if the light changed.

Ugh, this V.E.S.T.'s **driver** is out of date. And speaking of *driving...*

The top light still means **STOP** and the bottom one's **GO**, right?

COLE'S LAW: THE MUSICAL!

UPTOWN

SCREE

HONK

BEEP

VROOM

SCREE

*Very Exciting Spy Technology

5

General Inspector, it's a little hard to drive with your *FACE* blocking the road!

Oh, sorry!

Does it help if I duck down?

That reminds me, darling. Let's be sure our hotel pillows aren't **duck down**.

You're allergic to **goose** down, dear, not **duck**.

DUCK, GOOSE—

TAG! YOU'RE IT!

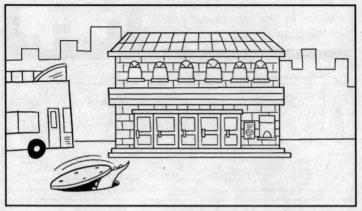

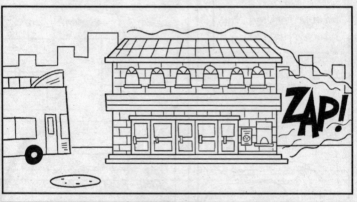

*Computerized Ocular Remote Butler

Shortly after...

GENERAL INSPECTOR

pat pat pat

MANGO AND **BRASH** REPORTING FOR DUTY, SIR!

InvestiGators, good.

Sorry, I'm having trouble with my TV. I can't get the picture to show up in **COLOUR.**

Anyway, last night someone *STOLE THE BANK!*

13

A couple of reverse-flushed toilets later...

COFFEE & CANS

"Have a pot, then hop on the pot"

Now *THIS* tastes like **cake**.

WHO SPLASHED **POTTY WATER** ALL OVER THE BATHROOM FLOOR?!

With us now is an **EYEWITNESS** who saw the *WHOLE THING!*

Really I only saw HALF. I'm a **ONE**-eyed witness!

I'm in town on *vay-cay*, as they say. At a **B&B** is where I stay!

I was about to have a light midnight snack, but was *disturbed* by a **strange rumblin'!**

What's that strange rumblin'?!

rumble rumble

I ran to the window in my **silk PJs** and saw a SHADOWY FIGURE levitatin' the bank with a **magic wand** or some such!

They's musta been some sorta **MAGICIAN!**

A MAGICIAN BANK ROBBER?

Could it have been **HOUDINO,** the dinosaur escape artist? His stage show was kinda *magician-adjacent.* Before he turned to *crime,* anyway.

Isn't he still locked up?

I've lost track, to be honest.

Plus, Houdino wouldn't have left behind so much **CASH.**

This thief took the building's worthless *BRICK* bricks, but left behind the valuable *GOLD* bricks!

IT'S DR. DOODLE— —DOO!

Dr. Doodledoo. See? I **knew** I'd get it.

But I Dr. Doodle**DON'T** believe it! Sure, he's a scientist who makes unsafe, unreliable, unregulated **laser beams,** but that's just how science is! It doesn't make him a **bad guy!** He's even helped *us* out in the past!

Bruh!

HEY! This **shadowy figure** you saw last night. Did they look like a BIG CHICKEN?

Meanwhile...

HOSPITAL

Just a nice, normal day at the hospital for ol' **Dr. Jake Hardbones**, brain surgeon.

It's all I've ever wanted since that very *UN-NORMAL* day I was *bitten* by that **rabid news helicopter!**

PEEK-A-BOO
ICU

RUMBLE RUMBLE

WHAT'S THAT RUMBLING?!

...into the *Action News Now* **HELICOPTER IN THE SKY!**

CHOO CHEE CHU CHI CHOO

HOSPITAL

As a **COPTER,** I'm compelled to report the news...

NEWS

...such as this figure below zapping the hospital with some kind of **LASER BEAM!**

vrrn

But as a **DOCTOR,** I must give aid to all the patients who need it in the hospital!!!

NEWS

HOSPITAL

vrrn

Such is the internal struggle of...**DOCTOR COPTER!**

27

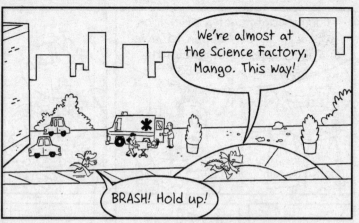

We're almost at the Science Factory, Mango. This way!

BRASH! Hold up!

Is it me, or was there a **hospital** here?

Dr. Hardbones?! What happened?

InvestiGators?

Someone...hijacked the hospital...with a **laser beam!**

Was it by any chance a rather **large chicken** who may have also stolen an entire **BANK?**

PLEASE! Don't say anything to me that's so **NEWSWORTHY!**

30

InvestiGators, Brash and Mango.

YUCK! Sounds *weird* when you say our names out of order like that.

We're looking for Dr. Doodledoo.

Sorry, he's out sick. Took off early yesterday.

Left plenty of himself *behind*, though...

Maybe there's better video footage here connecting him to the crime...

Can we see your security tapes?

I did this just yesterday with the city council! Dr. Doodledoo had gone home, so I stepped in as tour guide.

Why were they here?

There's an upcoming vote on city redistricting, and the factory might lose funding—

BOOORING! Show us the **COOL INVENTIONS** already!

Of course. This is Dr. Doodledoo's **LASER LAB.**

Doo's gotta lotta rays— *WAIT!* It looks like one is *missing...*

TICKLE RAY

POKE RAY

STING RAY

What's a **LEVITASER?**

LEVITASER

34

...buck buh—

BRUH?! What did I do?

You used your **LEVITASER** to steal an *ENTIRE BANK!*

WHAT? I'm just a normal chicken!

What do you mean, 'normal chicken'?

POLICE

I'm just an innocent chicken!

Then *WHY* are you dressed like a *BURGLAR?*

Because...

I'm **moulting.**

Our mission isn't over yet, Mango. We still need that chicken to *SQUAWK*, or we might never find the **missing buildings**.

InvestiGators! More buildings have *VANISHED!* You need to crack this case PRONTO! A **grocery store** floated into the sky only *FIVE MINUTES AGO!*

But...five minutes ago we were chasing Doodledoo through *THIS* building. How could he have *levitased THAT* building at the same time?

Hmm... TIME to rethink our **evidence**.

We only found ONE feather at the **bank**. And Dr. Doodledoo's been shedding them *EVERYWHERE*.

Yet we *DIDN'T* find a feather at the **hospital**. But I *DID* step on that **VOTE** badge... *JUST* like the ones we saw on the city council members!

Dr. Doodledoo left work yesterday morning, but according to the Head Scientist, the **levitaser** was *HERE* when the city council had their tour!

Sorry I'm late. I was, er...in the bathroom—

Here's the other one!

InvestiGators? What are you doing here?

BRASH! *WE* were *just* in the bathroom, and there was *NOBODY* else in there.

And *LOOK!*

No **VOTE** badge.

It must have been left at the *SCENE OF THE CRIME!*

I see. In that case, I'd like to call for this legislative session...

...TO BE A **LEVITATIVE SESSION!**

vrmm

45

But it's *MY* agenda! I spend **HOURS** in traffic commuting into the city...

It makes me see **RED!** *BUT NO LONGER!*

In fact...I kinda don't see *ANY* colour.

BANK

VRM

I just wanted all the places I like in town to be *closer* to my **house!**

SEE? There it is over there.

Hi, honey!

BANK

Why not just move your **house** into the **city?**

Do you know how much **CRIME** there is in the city?! Not even including the ones *I'VE* committed?

49

John Patrick Green is a *New York Times*–bestselling author who makes books about animals with human jobs, such as *Hippopotamister*, the Kitten Construction Company series, and the InvestiGators series. He is also the artist and co-creator of the Teen Boat! graphic novels with writer Dave Roman. John is definitely not just a bunch of animals wearing a human suit pretending to have a human job.

Christopher Hastings is a Brooklyn-based writer who is the creator of *The Adventures of Dr. McNinja* and co-creator of Marvel's *The Unbelievable Gwenpool*. He's worked on a slew of other comics like *Adventure Time*, *Five Nights at Freddy's*, and *I Am Groot*. He'll never tell you which gator is his favorite.

Pat Lewis is a freelance cartoonist/illustrator who lives in Pittsburgh, Pennsylvania, with his wife and their two cats. His artwork has appeared in children's magazines such as *Highlights* and *Scout Life*, as well as books by Workman Publishing, Macmillan, and McGraw Hill. Some of his favourite things in this world are: flea markets, road trips, monster movies, and snack-bar nachos.

BREAKING NEWS!
Join MANGO and BRASH for more awesome adventures, with COLOUR ARTWORK.

Investi GATORS A.N.T.S.

Investi GATORS Braver and Boulder

New York Times Bestselling Author
John Patrick Green

Investi GATORS Heist and Seek

New York Times Bestselling Author
John Patrick Green

Investi GATORS All Tide Up

John Patrick Green

An InvestiGators Adventure!
Agents of S.U.I.T.

"It's so funny I fell off my chair laughing."
Reader says 7+ on InvestiGators

John Patrick Green
with Christopher Hastings and Pat Lewis

Meet the InvestiGator's colourful coworkers!

An InvestiGators Adventure!
Agents of S.U.I.T.
From Badger to Worse

"It's so funny I fell off my chair laughing."
Reader says 7+ on InvestiGators

John Patrick Green
with Christopher Hastings and Pat Lewis

Happy
World Book Day!

When you've read this book, you can keep the fun going by swapping it, talking about it with a friend, or reading it again!

What do you want to read next? Whether it's **comics**, **audiobooks**, **recipe books** or **non-fiction** you can visit your school, local library or nearest bookshop for your next read – someone will always be happy to help.

SPONSORED BY

Changing lives through a love of books and reading.

World Book Day® is a charity sponsored by National Book Tokens

World Book Day is about changing lives through reading

When you **choose to read** in your spare time it makes you

Feel happier	**Better at reading**	**More successful**

Find your **reading superpower** by

1. **Listening to books being read aloud (or listening to audiobooks)**

2. **Having books at home**

3. **Choosing the books YOU want to read**

4. **Asking for ideas on what to read next**

5. **Making time to read**

6. **Finding ways to make reading FUN!**

ONSORED BY

Changing lives through a love of books and reading.

World Book Day® is a charity sponsored by National Book Tokens